Twin troubles

I love my wife Sarah very much and it's because she is always ready to make love at the drop of a hat. One night when I was horny and couldn't sleep because of my boner.

I cuddled up to Sarah with my hard-black cock on her big juicy white ass. I massaged her big titties, kissing her neck then I fingered her sweet white pussy until she was wet and ready.

Sarah moaned fuck me honey I'm wet in a sexy whisper. I tried to push my hard cock into Sarah's tight white pussy. It seemed tighter than normal so I forced my cock deep into her pussy.

Sarah moaned oh honey I love your big black cock deep in my white pussy. I rubbed Sarah's clit and fucked her hard. She fucking loved it, I gave it to her good

and Sarah went wild. I pulled out
of Sarah then climbed on top of
her. I entered her pussy again
giving her more cock.

Sarah held me tight and I fucked
her harder. She kissed me
passionately holding me tight. I
love when she holds me tight when
I pound her into the bed as I was
doing to her right now.

Sarah moaned and came on my cock
again. I said bend over goddess.
I smacked her sexy ass with my
hands than my hard cock with her
cream on it. I inserted my cock
firmly into her horny pussy again.

I pulled her long blonde hair and
fucked her hard. Sarah moaned yes
right there as I fucked the shit
out of her. She gave up the cream
yet again and a few seconds later.
I filled her pussy with all the

warm sperm that I had in both my
balls.

I said I love you so much baby,
you always give it up whenever I
need it. Sarah said oh yeah, I'm
happy to give it up to my stud
hubby anytime he needs some white
pussy. Sarah said I love you too
baby.

We went back to sleep holding
hands. I woke up when I heard two
voices in the kitchen. I put on
my robe and snuck up quietly. I
saw my wife Sarah and her sister
Shannon dressed alike chatting it
up.

I stood out of view and listened.
Sarah said did you enjoy my
husband's big black cock last
night. My eyes got wide and I
thought no wonder she felt
tighter. I was fucking my wife's
twin sister.

I thought oh wow that is so hot.
I fucking loved it. I continued
to listen. Shannon said oh my god
thank you so much for switching
with me last night.

She went on to say your husband is
a total stud he fucked the shit
out of me last night. The best
sex that I've ever had don't tell
my husband that I said that
against him.

Sarah said you like that big black
dick don't you sister. Shannon
said hell yeah, I'd do it again in
a heartbeat. Sarah said we can do
a switcheroo anytime. Shannon
said I loved when your husband
ejaculated his warm sperm into my
married white pussy.

Sarah said I love hearing that,
it's so hot. Shannon said we are
now stick sisters permanently.

The identical twins laughed out loud. That is when I walked in slowly. I said what are you two ladies laughing about, I said hey Shannon, good to see you. She hugged me tighter than normal and said it's great to see you too honey.

Sarah hugged and kissed me too, saying good morning honey breakfast is ready. All three of us sat down to eat in our robes. Both Sarah and her twin sister Shannon were looking at me and smiling.

I smiled at them too, I thought about my sperm being inside Shannon's naughty vagina and my wife approved of it, it blew my mind. I continued to pretend that I didn't know. I got ready for work. I left them to chat about me while I'm gone.

I came home and Shannon was still
there. She lives close by and is
always over to see her sister. I
don't mind hanging out with two
hot twins. We went to the living
room after dinner.

Shannon asked Sarah if she mind if
I cuddled with her since the air
conditioning was pretty cold. My
wife said sure go right ahead. I
don't mind, so we got under the
covers glued to each other.

Shannon said wow your husband is
so warm; my husband Steve isn't
this warm. Sarah said my
husband's wonderful muscles help a
lot. Shannon giggled and said it
doesn't hurt.

I held Shannon's hot ass close
with my cock glued to her big ass.
I became aroused rather quickly.
I decided to mess with her to see
if she would stop me. I slowly

massaged her big titties. I
expected her to stop me since her
twin was talking to her.

Shannon did nothing, so I
continued feeling on her melons
and grinding on her juicy ass. I
lifted up her dress to grind on
her wonderful ass. I rubbed her
pussy and it was wet as shit.

That is when I decided to fuck her
with my wife and her chatting it
up. I took my dick out putting my
cockhead on her pussy entrance. I
waited a second to see if she
would stop me and it never came so
I pushed and pushed until my black
cock was balls deep in her white
pussy.

I slowly fucked Shannon's married
white pussy. We both were quiet
as I fucked my wife's twin sister
right next to her. I felt Shannon
cream my cock a few times as I

fucked her slowly enjoying it
thoroughly.

Thirty minutes in and I ejaculated
my married sperm into my wife's
sister's pussy. Oh god I couldn't
believe it, I just came in
Shannon's pussy and she let me. I
kept my dick in her pussy until I
went soft then I took it out and
put it away.

The movie finished and Sarah asked
if Shannon was spending the night.
Both my wife and her sister are
web developers. They can work
from anywhere mostly at home. I'm
a web designer, Sarah makes more
than I do at 200K and me at 150K.

I'm working hard to get to her
level. But it's not working and I
have to live with it. We have a
great life in a great
neighborhood. It's just the

competitive nature in me to be
king.

Shannon said I'm staying the night
in the guest bedroom. We all got
up and were ready for bed.
Shannon hugged me tight and said
thanks for the warm cuddling. I
said my pleasure Shannon.

Sarah said are you warm now.
Shannon said oh yeah, I'm warm all
over now. Sarah and I laughed out
loud. Shannon smiled at both of
us. Sarah and I went to bed naked
as usual.

I was still horny so I climbed on
top of Sarah. I kissed her
passionately then sucked on her
big tits. I kissed my way down to
her clit. I bit and nibbled her
clit just like she likes it.

Sarah moaned oh honey fuck me with
your big black pole baby I need
it. I was happy to stick my dick
that I just took out of her sister
into her pussy. I held her hips
and fucked my wife.

Sarah moaned oh I love my husband
so much as she creamed my dirty
cock in her pussy. I said I love
you too my goddess fucking her
harder. Sarah said fuck me doggie
and fill me with your warm sperm.
I said my pleasure sexy wifey.

Sarah bent over and jiggled her
big booty. I smacked it and enter
her pussy again. Sarah watched me
in the mirror on our bed as I
fucked her hard. I said I love
fucking my hot wife doggie. Sarah
said I love getting drilled by my
horny husband.

I fucked her harder and harder as
her ass jiggled on me. I moaned

and my eyes rolled back in my head
as I filled my Sarah with my warm
sperm. Sarah said oh yeah baby I
love when you cum in my white
pussy. It makes this white girl
feel great every time. I said I
love spilling my seed in you baby.

We kissed cuddled and went to
sleep. A week later, Sarah and
Shannon along with me were in our
bed watching our 75-inch 4K QLED
Samsung television. With us three
under the covers next to each
other. I decided to use my middle
fingers by rubbing both of their
sweet white pussies.

I went even further by inserting
my middle fingers in both of their
sweet white pussies. Both were
biting their lips as I fingered
their wet pussies. I felt their
vibrations in both of their
pussies on both my hands. It was
very exhilarating to make both of

them cum at the same time. I felt
godlike doing so.

Sarah told Shannon that she could
sleep here tonight. Shannon said
that works for me. I didn't want
to go back to the guest room.

We talked for a while then went to
sleep lovingly. I woke up during
the night and started fingering
Sarah. She woke up when her pussy
became wet then said get on top
and fucked me while my sister
sleeps next to us. Sarah had a
big smile on her pretty face. I
kissed her and entered her balls
deep.

I fucked Sarah vigorously and she
loved it. We were in our own
little world fucking like bunnies.
When Shannon woke up and turned on
the light. She said oh my god you
two are fucking. Sarah said sorry
sister, my husband wanted some

pussy and I never say no to his
big black cock. An orgasm hit
Sarah and she screamed out loud.

I said bend over sweet cheeks.
Sarah bent over and Shannon saw my
cock penetrating her sister.
Shannon said oh my god that is a
big fucking black cock.

Sarah said oh yeah and it gives me
multiple orgasm every time we
fuck. Shannon said it is a
beautiful cock. Sarah said you
like it don't you, after he cums
in me. If you can get him hard
again, you can fuck him too.

Shannon said oh yeah, I've always
wanted some black dick in my white
pussy. I smacked Sarah's fat ass
and fucked her harder. I pulled
her hair and pounded her hard
until I felt a tingle in my balls.
I let my sperm go into my kinky

wife moaning with immense
pleasure.

Sarah said oh yeah, he came in me,
I love it every time. Shannon
said my turn as my cock went soft.
She took her night gown off as I
watched revealing her naked body
to my drooling eyes. Shannon
grabbed my cock and stroked it
while massaging my balls. My cock
came back to life, Sarah said oh
yeah, it's back and Shannon said I
knew I could get it up.

Shannon laid down and said you may
enter giggling. I kissed her
passionately then I sucked her big
tits as she moaned. I kissed my
way down to her pussy. I fingered
her pussy and sucked on her clit.

Shannon moaned oh god Sarah your
husband is a wonderful pussy
eater. I tried to enter her pussy
but she was still tight as hell.

Sarah said force it in that married pussy.

I pushed harder until I filled Shannon up balls deep. I started pumping Shannon's white pussy full of black cock. Shannon said oh my god my first black cock. I said my pleasure baby as I fucked her harder and harder. Shannon moaned as she lubricated my cock with her pussy cream. Sarah said oh yeah cum on my husband's big black cock.

I said bend over sister in law, time for doggie. Shannon said oh yeah, I love doggie too. I smacked her cheeks as she jiggled her ass. I plunged my love dagger into her white pussy again.

Sarah smacked Shannon's ass then said take my husbands married cock up your married cunt. I fucked her harder and harder. Shannon

said pull my hair baby. I pulled
her blonde hair and gave it to her
strong.

Shannon's pussy vibrated and
creamed my bone. I moaned a
minute later and filled my sister
in law with warm sperm. I said oh
wow Sarah did you like me creaming
your sister. Sarah said oh yeah,
I love it. She kissed me and
Shannon said that was the best sex
that I've ever had with a man.
I've never creamed a dick that
many times before while getting
fucked.

I said my pleasure Shannon. Sarah
said so you would give it up to my
husband again. Shannon said hell
yeah, your husband can fuck me
anytime his dick gets hard. I'd
never say no like you sister.

Sarah said that does it, we are
officially stick sisters. They

started laughing then hi fived
each other. I smiled lovingly at
the fact that I was fucking two
hot twins.

A month into me fucking Sarah and
her sister whenever I wanted. It
was a Saturday afternoon in our
hood. Sarah said she needed a nap
then Shannon said let's go for a
walk around the hood. I said ok,
we put on our walking shoes then
went for a walk. We ran into
Heather the next-door neighbor.
Shannon said call me Sarah I'll
pretend I'm her when talking to
Heather.

I said hi Heather and she hugged
me tight like she usually does
then she said hi Sarah and hugged
her too. We started shooting the
shit when Shannon said I love
being married to a black man. I
get unlimited black cock in my
white pussy. I said thanks Sarah
that is nice of you to say.

Heather said oh wow unlimited
black cock that is something
special. Shannon said you've had
some black dick haven't you
Heather. Heather looked at me bit
her lips then said no I haven't
had the pleasure of a black man on
top of me balls deep in my white
pussy.

Shannon said oh boy you don't know
what you're missing. Heather said
tell me about it, I'm married to a
white guy not much chance for a
black cock in me. Shannon said
sorry Heather maybe next lifetime.
Heather said definitely with a
giggle.

We hugged goodbye and went back
home. Sarah was awake as we came
back. She said how was the walk.
I said Shannon pretended to be you
with Heather and I told her the
whole story.

Sarah said oh my god Shannon, she
really likes my husband. Shannon
said would she fuck your husband
if you let her. I said no way she
is a good girl. Sarah said that
would be hot, I'll invite her
over.

I said that should be fun. The
following weekend, Heather came
over in a little black dress. I
was turned on and Sarah talked her
into watching television in our
bed.

Sarah is really good at persuading
people to see things her way. I
took my shirt off and Heather
couldn't take her eyes off me.
Sarah had the biggest smile on her
face. I was hard and ready. I
took my boxers off under the
covers so I was naked and ready.

Sarah took the covers off and said
look Heather. She looked and said

oh my god that's a big black cock.
I said thank you Heather, she said
your welcome. Sarah said go ahead
and stroke it. I don't mind,
Heather said what the hell then
started stroking my black cock. I
moaned enjoying it thoroughly.

Heather said oh my god I can't
believe I'm stroking your
husband's big cock, Sarah. My
wife said I don't mind; do you
want to get on it. Heather said
oh yeah, she looked at me took her
dress off with nothing under it
and mounted my cock.

Heather held it firm and slid her
tight white married pussy down my
black pole. I moaned oh god
Heather, I can't believe I'm balls
deep in your little white pussy.
I've always fantasized about
fucking your white pussy. Heather
said I've fantasized about getting
fucked by your big black cock too.

Sarah said the feelings are mutual now fuck my husband like you mean it bitch smacking her fat ass. Heather fucked me harder as I squeezed her big titties. I pulled her down and kissed her passionately. She returned to fucking me with a big smile on her face moaning as she creamed my cock for the first time.

I rolled her over so I could fuck her missionary. I fucked her hard from above as she creamed my bone again. I pulled out and bent her over. Sarah kissed me as I entered Heather and said I love watching you fuck other white bitches.

I pulled Heather's long black hair and pounded her pussy properly. Heather said oh my god I love your black cock deep in my white pussy as she came again. I smacked her ass and give her more until I

squirted all the sperm I had in my
penis into her married pussy.

I said oh wow Heather thanks for
the married pussy. Heather said
no thank you for my first black
cock, I appreciate this more than
you know. Shannon burst in the
door with me still in Heather.
She said oh my god, you stud,
fucking the neighbor. Heather
said oh my god you have an
identical twin.

Sarah said sorry it was her
talking dirty to you today.
Heather's eyes got big. Shannon
said I love when your husband
calls me Sarah, I said kinky
sister in law. Sarah said you can
call me Shannon when you fuck me
next time. Shannon said you can
call me Sarah next time you fuck
me too.

Heather said oh wow you fucked her
too. I said oh yeah, Sarah
doesn't mind me fucking her sister
or the hot neighbor. Sarah smack
Heather's big ass and said if you
want some more black dick in your
little twat come on over baby.
Heather said I'll be over a lot
more when my husband is gone for
months at a time.

I said ok my little sluts, I need
to get to sleep. I kissed all
three and went to sleep. Monday,
I went to work early. My boss
Sharon was in her office. I said
good morning boss. She was
wearing a short ass skirt and a
cleavage top. I said wow boss you
look great today.

Sharon said I know it's a little
slutty but I felt naughty this
morning so I put it on. I was
already hard checking her out.
Sharon hugged me tight and I
couldn't help myself. I grabbed

her big juicy ass and squeezed.
Sharon moaned and said oh god that
feel so good baby don't stop.

I lifted up her skirt to feel her
bare ass. Sharon kissed me
passionately oh my god it was on.
She said do you want to fuck the
boss I'm horny and we are the only
ones here. I said hell yeah.

She took my hand and we went to
the couch. Sharon laid down and I
mounted her. I pushed and pushed
until I was able to penetrate her
tight ass white pussy with my
black penis. I said oh my god I'm
finally in you, boss.

She said oh yeah now pound me with
that big black bone. I squeezed
her big ass tits and fucked her
like a savage. Sharon moaned oh
god I'm creaming that big fucking
dick. I said oh god yeah as I
felt her lubrication. I redoubled

my efforts giving her the
business. Sharon came again as I
fucked her harder.

We both heard a knock on the door
and Megan's voice. Sharon smiled
at me and said come on in Megan.
Sharon bent over and I was about
to enter her doggie. Megan said
oh wow you two are fucking and you
have a really big black cock.

I started fucking Sharon hard as
shit as Megan watched biting her
lips and rubbing her sweet white
thighs together. Sharon said oh
god here it comes again. I felt
her pussy vibrate then a lot of
lubrication. Sharon said oh wow
that was the big one.

She said pull out and I did,
Sharon said I know you want some
Megan here is your shot and Megan
said but I'm married. I sat down

stroking my penis as she watches
it with passion in her eyes.

Megan said what the hell,
straddling me holding my dick and
sliding her married white pussy
down my black pole. I said oh god
your tight as shit, Megan said
your big as shit, bigger than my
husband don't tell him I said that
baby.

Megan started riding my cock hard
and fast with a lot of passion.
Sharon said Megan's always told me
she wanted some black in her every
time she sees your muscles.

I sucked her big tits and bit her
nipples as she fucked the shit out
of my cock. Megan moaned out loud
and came all over my cock. I said
that's my girl Megan. I bent her
over and took her from behind.
Sharon said oh my god that's hot
as I fucked the shit out of Megan.

I couldn't hold it any longer and
I let myself go deep in Megan's
tight ass married vagina. I said
oh god that was amazing fucking
the boss and her secretary in the
same day. Sharon said did you
like fucking our married vaginas.

I said hell yeah no better way to
start the day. Megan said thanks
for the cock always wanted some
black in me. Sharon said me too
baby. I hugged and kissed both of
them. We straighten up and got
ready for a full day of work.

I called my wife Sarah and told
her that I fucked Sharon my boss
and her secretary Megan. Sarah
said oh my god that is so hot, I
wish I could have seen that baby.
I said I wish you were here too my
little kinky wifey. Sarah said I
love you and I heard Shannon said
I love you too stud. I said I
love you too Shannon.

Later that day when I left to go
home. I enter the house and Sarah
jumped on me totally naked. I
fell against the wall; I undid my
pants it fell and I slid Sarah
down my cock. She moaned and said
call me Shannon baby. I said oh
yeah Shannon fuck my cock.

We kissed and I fucked Shannon
hard. She came when I called her
Shannon again. I spun her around
pinned her hands on the wall and
hammered her kinky ass. I moaned
and filled Shannon with my warm
seed. We kissed and held each
other as we panted for breath. I
said that was intense baby. I
smacked her juicy ass then she
laid on the couch trying to
recover.

I went to our bedroom and the real
Shannon was there naked. She said
I hope you still have juice for
your wifey. I said I always have
juicy for my wifey Sarah. She

moaned and said oh yeah. She saw
my cock get hard again then said
get on top baby. I squeezed her
big fucking titties and entered
her deep.

I started pounding and she started
moaning. I moaned oh Sarah I love
your tight pussy wifey. I held
her shoulders and fucked the shit
out of her. She flooded my cock
with her cream 10 seconds before I
filled her with my seed.

I kissed her and the real Sarah
behind us said welcome home baby.
I hope you loved our warm welcome.
I said best welcome home all year
as fake Sarah and I lay back
trying to recover from an intense
fucking.

All three of us fell asleep and
woke up for dinner. We ate and
showered then went back to sleep
as a threesome.

Three months later, I was in Sharon's office talking to her when Megan came in and told me that she was having my baby and it is a boy. I said oh no that's when her cell rang and it was her husband. Megan answered it and said he wants to talk to you.

I said oh boy, Megan said no its ok take it. I took the phone and her husband said thanks for impregnating my wife, we have been trying for 5 years so thank you for helping us become a complete family. I said you're welcome I'm glad you're not mad. He said we wanted to be parents, it doesn't matter how it happened, we both are very happy and over the moon with joy.

I said I'm happy for both of you and he hung up. Megan hugged and kissed me thanking me for knocking her up. Sharon said congrats, I was a witness to conception. She hugged and kissed me congratulating me. I said thanks boss. She hugged and congratulated Megan too.

Megan left and went back to her desk. Sharon said you stud you're going to be a daddy. I said oh yeah, I can't wait to tell my wife. Sharon said isn't she going to be mad. I said no, she knows I fucked you and Megan. Sharon said oh wow, she is a kinky one. I said you have no idea. She lets me fuck her twin sister Shannon, and the hot next-door neighbor Heather.

Sharon said oh wow, I love your wife. I said I love her too. During lunch I called and told Sarah the news. She was very excited and said I can't wait to babysit your baby with Megan.

I went home and I was on the couch
hanging out with Sarah and Shannon
when Heather came over. She said
I have some news for all of you.
Heather said she is pregnant and
having my son. I said oh my god
that is great, I'm happy for us
but what about your husband.
Heather said I'll just tell him
it's his son. I said that could
work.

Sarah said congratulations on
having a son with my husband. I
can't wait to babysit my husband's
son. Shannon said I can't wait to
babysit my lovers son with the hot
neighbor and we all laughed.

Six months later, Heather and
Megan were due around the same
time. Megan's son Mark came out
first. I was there in the
hospital all nervous. Her husband
came out and gave me the good news
that mother and son are ok. We

hugged and had a good cry
together.

We went into the room and Megan
said are you two crying. Her
husband said allergies and we all
laughed out loud. I met my son
and held him close. It felt
surreal and wonderful.

A week later I was at the same
hospital, with Heather since her
husband was out of the country and
couldn't make it back in time.
After a few hours of labor, Marty
was born healthy and happy while
screaming his head off. His lungs
were working no problem.

Heather's husband made it the next
day so I left them alone and the
baby looked white enough to pass
as their baby but it was mine.

When her husband left, she brought
the baby over to meet, Shannon and
Sarah. We played with the baby
and gave Heather a break since she
was a stay at home mom with her
hubby bring home a lot of bacon.

Heather felt guilty and told her
husband that I knocked her up and
surprisingly he was ok with it.
They apparently were told by the
doctors that Heather couldn't have
kids so both were happy to have a
baby even if it was with me.
Apparently, Heather's husband
knows of her black cravings and
I'm very cool with her cravings.

Sarah persuaded Megan and Heather
to let her babysit my kids from
time to time. That made me a very
happy father. Shannon was happy
to have the kids over too and she
loved playing with the kids too.

When they got older, Sarah bought
and expensive playground set for
our backyard. The boys loved it,
we had to drag them from it on
many occasions to eat or go home.

We loved playing in the backyard.
Many years later, we had to sit
them down and tell them how they
came to be. They took it rather
well, I bought them both cars for
their 18th birthday. I was happy
when Heather and Megan along with
their husbands didn't get upset.

My two sons were good friends form
playing together and going to the
same prep school that we all paid
for together including my horny
boss Sharon. I was a proud papa
when they both graduated along
with their twin girlfriends. I
was there with Shannon and Sarah
along with Megan, Heather and
their husbands.

Sarah asked me during the graduation Ceremony, I wander if my son's identical twin girlfriend Tori and Lori ever pulled a switcheroo. I said I don't want to know then I thought about it and then I asked Sarah. Did you and your sister ever pull a switcheroo on me. Sarah said yes please don't be mad and I said I love that you did it to me. Sarah said I love you and I know you're as kinky as me. I smiled at my loving wife and kissed her on her blow job lips.

I was happy when both my son's wanted to go to MIT, alma mater of Shannon, Sarah and me. They also wanted to be near their twin girlfriends going to Harvard.

The end